It's a King's Life
in
Phoenix

Written by Emily Randolph
Photo Illustrations by Dan Merchant

A proud endeavor of

happy LADY productions

Scottsdale

About the Author & Artist

Emily and Dan left their long-term careers in marketing to combine their love of dogs and storytelling with a way to give back and get involved in their community. They started by donating a children's picture book, *Dogs Are... Just Like You!*, to Phoenix pet therapy charity, Gabriel's Angels.

From there, the idea took seed. Emily could do what she loves – writing – and Dan could do what he loves – photography – and together, they could publish books that help animal welfare and pet therapy programs through a combination of messaging and personal charitable efforts. A substantial portion of all their sales goes to charity.

Emily is the author of the *King's Life* series; *Dogs Are... Just Like You!*; *Dima's Dog School, The Foolproof New Way to Train Your Dog*; and *Handfeeding Handbook, 5 Easy Steps to a Well-Trained, Happy Dog*.

Dan has nurtured a passion for photography all his life. His credits include: the *King's Life* series, *Limericks by The Brothers Randolph* and *Some Days You're the Dog... Some Days, the Hydrant!*

––––––––––––––––––––––

ISBN-13: 978-1482000153
ISBN-10: 1482000156

Foreword

Happy and Lady of *It's a King's Life in Carmel-by-the-Sea* recently adopted a new sister, Lucy, a ruby red Cavalier King Charles Spaniel, from the Cavalier Rescue Foundation in Phoenix. Turns out, Lucy is a ball of fire and Happy and Lady need to find things for her to do! *It's a King's Life in Phoenix* introduces Lucy to all the great adventures to be had every day all year round, right in her backyard.

In our story 'Phoenix' is defined as the entire Valley of the Sun, and we have included our favorite dog-friendly places in the towns of Scottsdale, Gilbert, Phoenix, South Phoenix and Paradise Valley. Please refer to our **Resource Guide** at the back of the book for more ideas on great places to go with your dog. By no means is this list exhaustive; it simply represents our personal four-paw recommendations. It's up to you to...
Sniff out adventure!

Once upon a time... in fact, this very day,
there is a little dog named Lucy.

Lucy is very red and very curious.

She also has a habit of getting into mischief
at her home in Phoenix.
Toilet paper, in fact, is a favorite toy.
And you know what else?

Flower pots. Yes, flower pots! Lucy loves the way the flowers smell. She loves the way they taste. And she loves how the earth feels as it sinks between her toes.

Her sister, Lady, and her brother, Happy, however, are not amused. Every day they bark, "Lucy, please get out of the flower pots!"

Lady, Lucy and Happy talk for hours about all the things they could do.
Why, they realize, there is fun for every season in Phoenix:
spring, summer, fall and winter.
All they have to do is follow their noses and... sniff out adventure.

READY

SET

SNIFF!

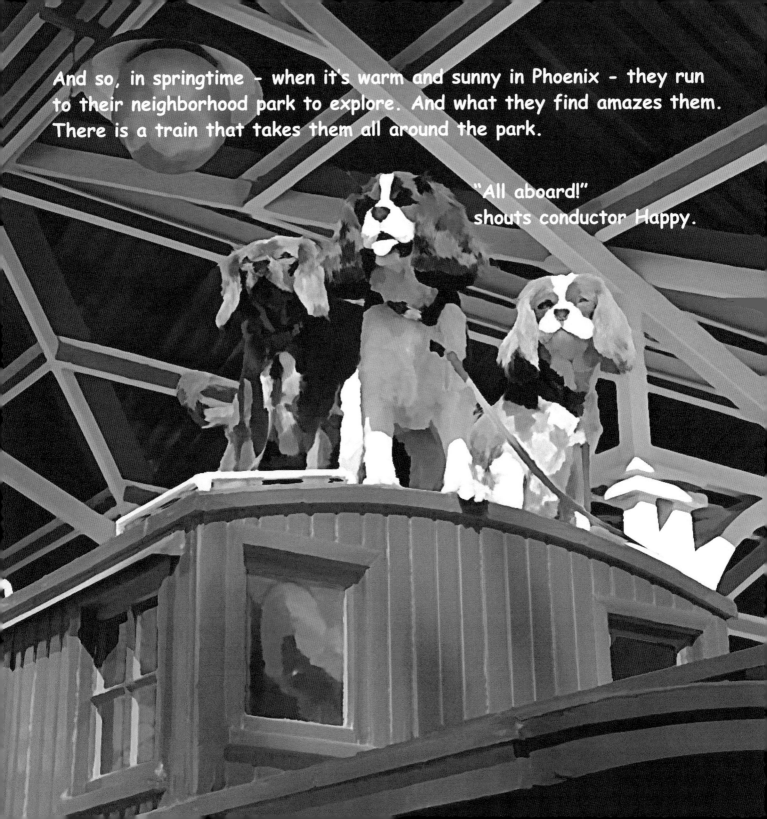

And so, in springtime - when it's warm and sunny in Phoenix - they run to their neighborhood park to explore. And what they find amazes them. There is a train that takes them all around the park.

"All aboard!" shouts conductor Happy.

There's even a stagecoach. Lady and Lucy dream about how life was back in the Old Wild West...

Bumpy, probably.

And on other spring days, all three dogs follow their noses to find lip-smacking outdoor cafés.

You know what? They always clean their plates.

Phoenix is known as 'The Valley of the Sun.' Why?
Because it's sunny here almost every single day.

Springtime is especially perfect to walk through all the outdoor
markets and stroll amongst the shops.

But, very red and very curious Lucy still likes playing in the
flower pots best.
Happy and Lady are not amused. What do they say?
"Lucy, please get out of the flower pots."

Spring is also wonderful for hiking - like climbing to the top of majestic Camelback Mountain.

Happy feels like the 'King of the World' looking over his hometown.

And as they hike up and up and up, the dogs discover that Camelback overlooks a world-famous resort with beautiful green golf courses. What a view!

After they reach the summit, Happy, Lady and Lucy race down the mountain - 12 paws flying - to visit the property.

To their surprise, they are offered a special tour aboard the resort's special Bear Buggy.

Where will they go?

Their first stop is to a blue lagoon to feed the koi - very beautiful, colorful fish that are nearly as large as Lady.

There, they meet Phoe-Phoe (fo-fo), the resort's furry mascot. See her white cottontail?

After visiting the koi, Phoe-Phoe takes them for a stroll through the resort's cactus garden. The cacti come in all shapes and sizes and have many interesting names, like Queen Victoria, Prickly Pear and Big Tooth. They sit a spell to rest and enjoy the scenery.

"Listen very carefully," whispers Phoe-Phoe in Lady's ear. "I have a very special treat in store for all of you next."

What a surprise! Phoe-Phoe invites them to dine on the 8th tee of the resort's golf course - right where golfers tee up to hit to the far green. With a view as far as the eye can see, dinner is very elegant. What is Phoe-Phoe nibbling on for her meal?

Lady, Happy and Lucy have had quite a spring! But soon, it gets very hot. How hot? Oven hot. Summer is the best time for swimming in the family pool...

And visiting their favorite 'beach' just for woofs. Yes, desert Phoenix has a dog beach and lake.

Very red and very curious Lucy tries to keep up with big brother Happy, while Lady ponders her reflection.

Can you see her nose in the water?

On other summer days, they visit their pal Nigel, who runs one of the best pet toy stores!

On another summer day, they
follow their noses north to cool
Sedona - home of the Red Rocks -
to go hiking and play in the park.

Sedona
Dog Park
Hiking Area / Hilly Terrain

Can you see Lucy?
She almost gets lost in all
the red earth.

After running in the park and up and down trails, they really need a bath! Luckily, gentle Oak Creek river is the perfect bathtub to soak their paws, followed by a dunk in a bucket of fresh water, of course.

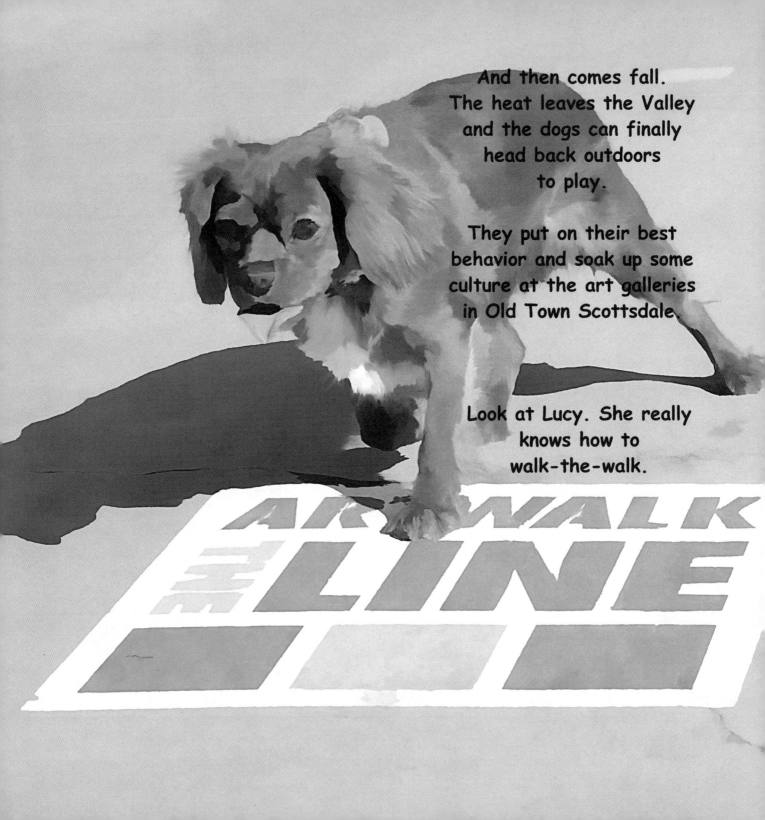

And then comes fall.
The heat leaves the Valley
and the dogs can finally
head back outdoors
to play.

They put on their best
behavior and soak up some
culture at the art galleries
in Old Town Scottsdale.

Look at Lucy. She really
knows how to
walk-the-walk.

And Lady loves all the beautiful statues that remind visitors of how the West was settled.

And, it's perfect weather to visit many of the nearby resorts. Many organize dog parties, host dog shows and offer special menus. Best of all, they encourage their canine visitors to relax and lounge.

Happy, Lady and Lucy just
love the resorts.
Maybe, too, it's because
many are so very generous
with their doggie treats.

And, yet, very red and very curious Lucy seeks more adventure. She's still up to her old tricks. Happy and Lady are not amused. What do they shout? "Lucy, please get out the flower pots!"

Winter quickly follows fall, and so it's time to prepare for the holidays. All three dogs book appointments at the spa.

Happy has a paw massage with butter balm.
Lucy gets her red coat conditioned.
And Lady has her hair clipped and styled.
Doesn't she look luxurious in her pink spa bathrobe?

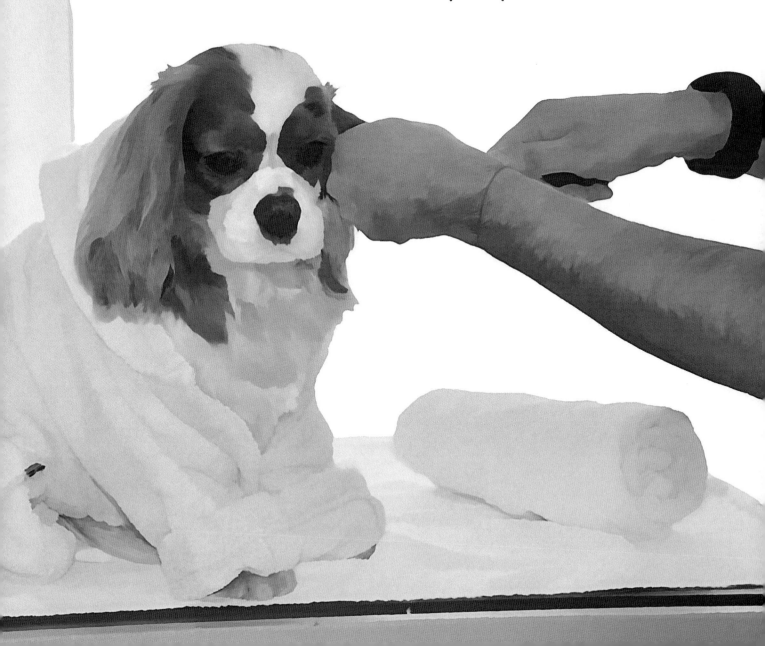

She even does 'doga'
- doggy yoga -
to get in shape.
Stretch it, Lady!

At last, all groomed, they are ready for the holidays.

They choose a cozy inn with lovely gardens to celebrate their wonderful year.

Amazingly, instead of playing
in the flower pots, very red
and very curious Lucy wants
to play ball, instead.

Happy shows her how it's done. Look at him jump!

Lady prefers to stroll in the gardens, smell the flowers and enjoy the lovely sculptures. While she wanders, she wonders if Lucy enjoyed her year of adventures in Phoenix.

Indeed, Lucy has. "I loved every day! Who knew there is so much to do and discover right at home," she says.

Not surprisingly, they are all very tired after a big year of fun. What do you think they are dreaming about?

Yes, you are right! All the great new adventures still to come. All they have to do is...

Phoenix Resource Guide
For Dog Lovers

Animal Rescue
Arizona Animal Welfare League
Arizona Humane Society
Cavalier Rescue Trust
Cavalier Rescue Foundation

Art
Scottsdale Art Walk

Dog Parks*
Cosmo's Dog Park

Dog & Kid's Park
McCormick Ranch Railroad

Dog Spa & Grooming
Oh My Dog! Boutique & Spa
Grooming Tails

Hiking
Camelback Mountain
McDowell Sonoran Preserve
Papago Park
Phoenix Mountain Preserve
Tempe Town Lake

Pet Boutique
Mackie's Parlour

Pet Therapy
Gabriel's Angels

Resorts**
Arizona Biltmore
Firesky Resort & Spa
Four Seasons Scottsdale
The Hermosa Inn
Hyatt Regency Scottsdale
Montelucia Resort & Spa
The Phoenician (home of Phoe-Phoe)***
Pointe Hilton Resorts
The Radisson Ft. McDowell
The Westin Kierland
W Scottsdale

Restaurants & Cafés
Zinc Bistro
The Farm at South Mountain
The Herb Box
Paradise Bakery
Starbucks
Veneto Trattoria

Sedona Day Trip
Sedona Dog Park
Slide Rock State Park
L'Auberge de Sedona
Tlaquepaque Arts & Crafts
Rene's restaurant

Shopping
Biltmore Fashion Park
Kierland Commons
Scottsdale Quarter

Vet
Richard Stolper, DVM
Scottsdale Ranch
Animal Hospital

*Nearly every community has off-leash dog park(s). Cosmo's is particularly great for water-loving woofs.

**Phoenix has many dog-friendly hotels. Please call ahead for pet policies and programs, as they are subject to change.

*** Stay tuned for more adventures with Phoe-Phoe!

Know of other great dog-friendly places?
Let us know on: Facebook.com/HappyLadyProductions

It's a King's Life.®

Sniff out adventure!

More in the series:
It's a King's Life in Carmel-by-the-Sea
It's a Ling's Life in Aspen (Nov. 2013)

Happy Lady Productions, LLC (HLP) is an independent, philanthropic publisher of non-fiction, fiction and children's picture books created by husband and wife team, photographer and photo illustrator Dan Merchant and writer Emily Randolph. HLP donates to animal rescue and pet-therapy charities.

Titles include: *It's a King's Life* series; *Dogs Are...Just Like You!; Handfeeding Handbook: 5 Easy Steps to a Well-Trained, Happy Dog; Some Days You're the Dog... Some Days, the Hydrant!; and Limericks by The Brothers Randolph.*

Please contact us for more information:
HappyLadyProductions.com

18087930R00021

Made in the USA
Charleston, SC
15 March 2013